Vivid

Erotic Short Stories

Vivid

Vivid

Erotic Short Stories
Revised Edition

Jenae' Jones
Southern Lady Books
2016

Vivid

Vivid

Copyright © 2015 by J. Jones

All rights reserved. This book or any portion thereof may not be reproduced or used in any manner whatsoever without the express written permission of the publisher except for the use of brief quotations in a book review or scholarly journal.

First Printing: 2015

Southern Lady Books
LaVergne, TN. 37086

Dedication

I dedicate this to him, my best friend,
the one that makes me smile.
I love you to life. Thank you for always
supporting me in everything I do and try to do.
For being my number one fan.
Thank you for encouraging me to take my shot.
You always know what to say that's your gift.
Love, Me
"No Shoes Shawty"

Vivid

The Stories...

Acknowledgements
Introduction
Come On In
Cozy Night In
Day and Night....the next day
Put In Work
Reflections
Long Distance
A Memory
To Reconcile

Acknowledgements

I never thought my passion for writing would ever combine with my love for most things erotic. I'm thankful for my friends that saw in me what I was afraid to see in myself.
To my senior English teacher Mrs. Huff, who was the first adult I can remember telling me I had a talent with words, thank you for speaking those words into my life.
Thank you in advance to everyone that enjoys my expression.
If you keep buying, I promise to keep writing.

Vivid

Introduction

Dear Tyrone,

I've missed you so much and look forward to the day you walk back through my door.

Wrapping my arms around you is something I can't wait to do. Kissing you while melting into your big strong arms and feeling secure and sexy as you hold me is something that excites me. It's been months since I've felt you. It's been too long since you held me. The fantasy of it all is my escape of our reality. Knowing we are what we are and where we are is hard at times but dreaming of what we could be and where we could end up makes it wet. The idea of being with no other man ever in life turns me on. To know I can freely fuck you is refreshing. Imagining the day you walk into our home and take me while in the kitchen with no words spoken makes me drip. Feeling you in my sleep from behind makes my body tingle. Picturing me on top of you in the mirror as I ride you makes my kitty purr. To climax together is satisfying. No pull outs, no barriers, no stopping. Hair pulling and juices flowing. Easy glides inside a tight space. Hands gripping and nails scratching. Ass bouncing and hips grinding. Nipple biting. Passionate kissing and eye gazing. I've missed you so much and look forward to the day you walk back through my door.

Love, Kayla

Come On In...

    The ringing of the doorbell signaled that something special was about to happen. She walked to the door excited about who stood on the other side. As the door opened wider, so did his eyes. They glanced at her sexiness, which was framed by the door way. The purple pumps on her feet forced the curves of her legs to stand out. The purple added a nice pop of color to the silky black robe that fell to the form of her womanhood. He looked her up and down and admired her attention to detail as only peeks of her soft brown skin were exposed. She stepped back and he stepped in. She took him by the hand and lead him through the candlelit hall way. The sway of her robe teased him as he walked behind her. Unwilling to wait for the bedroom, he turned her towards him and pulled her in for a kiss. The passion between their lips filled the room. He bent her over the arm of the couch and created a perfect arch in her back. He began to kiss up her legs. Starting from her ankles, his hands gripped her waist and caressed her hips. Like a man climbing up the curves of a mountain, he held her firmly. Before he reached her peaks, his tongue dipped into the river of her cave. His hands palmed her ass while he ate her from behind. The echoes of her moans were suffocated by the cushions of the couch…..

Vivid

Cozy Night In...

Tyrone was standing over the sink washing dishes while Kayla sat on the sofa working away on her laptop. The soft glow of the screen made only her face visible to him.

"What are you working on?" he asked from the kitchen into the open den. She looked up for a second and then back down at her screen, "these final budget reports for my client", was her response.

In that moment, it was a turn on for him to hear her talk about work. She was the owner of a successful consulting firm and her being the boss was sexy to him.

He finished the dishes and then decided to join her on the couch for a moment of peace. As he sat there, she could sense that he desired her attention. She closed her laptop and placed it on the coffee table. She moved closer to him and rested her head on his chest. It was then that he noticed that she must have changed clothes after dinner, while he was cleaning the kitchen. She had cooked dinner and he thought it was only fair to clean up for her. She stretched out next to him in her custom KOS t-shirt and boy shorts. The tv was on but they weren't really paying attention anymore.

His fingers softly slid across her shoulders to stimulate her senses and they began a casual conversation. As she laid with her head resting on his chest, he transferred the warmth of his touch through her body.

As Tyrone reflected on the week he had, he suddenly became grateful for her presence and decided to show her just how much he loved her. Being careful not to completely shift her from her position of comfort, he moved her legs onto his lap. He took his time to rub away the worries of her day. She laid back and fell deeper into the comfort zone.

As he admired the look of peace on her face, he took advantage of her openness. He moved up her legs, pressing firmly inch by inch to relax the muscles that formed the sexiness of her stance. Once he passed the midpoint of her legs, she allowed his hands to glide across the softness of her thighs. He massaged over and under the curves that controlled the switch in her walk. In her mind she knew where his next stop would be. The place that only he could call his but to her surprise, he paid it no mind. Instead he focused on the places that held her back from full relaxation.

He slowly positioned her body to be able to reach her lower back with his firm and gentle caress. His hands moved up and down and side to side. She began to fall into a space where nothing else mattered. Just before sleep could take over, there was the cooling surprise of his tongue on her neck. It opened her eyes but wasn't shocking enough to move her body. He slowly and softly kissed away the remains of her tension. He could feel her body melt in his hands. The restrictions of the couch forced him to move the moment. He wanted to have his way with her softness and needed room to play.

He led her by the hand to the bedroom and watched as she crawled into their king size playground. He observed how the dip in her back complimented the rise and turns of her curves.

She laid down on her stomach awaiting his next move. Suddenly she felt the heat of his body covering the coolness of her fully exposed backside. His tongue tickled directly down the center of her back. As he reached the nape of her ass, there was a shift in her posture. He knew it was time to remind her why she was the woman and he was the man. He grabbed her hips and raised them to the appropriate level off the bed and then whispered, "Don't move".

He slid underneath her into a position that brought his lips closer to the lips of her hips. He kissed the middle of her body holding on tightly to her waist. Her sounds started to escape the pillow that held her face. He wanted to tell her he loved her but didn't speak the words into her ears. Minutes into his expression he could taste the fact that she heard him.

As her appreciation for his love dripped down his chin he knew it was only a matter of time before she took control and reminded him he wasn't alone in this.

Before he had a chance to position her again, he was on his back and was looking down at the top of her head. She wanted to drink his love and was careful not to waste it. She started to suck on him as if she was trying to get the taste of a thick milkshake and only his chocolate straw could fulfill her thirst. Each up and down motion brought him closer to melting in her mouth. She could tell and slowed down.

Between licking her tongue from top to bottom, she was able to speak softly, "Not yet....I want to taste.....all of you."

Kayla kissed, licked, and sucked all the sensitive places that brought pleasure to him. As Tyrone drifted deeper into his zone there was a sudden pause in the playtime. He opened his eyes to the pleasant surprise of her standing at the foot of the bed. The moonlight highlighted her skin and she whispered "Where do you want me, sir?"

He stared at her, visually taking all of her in and said, "on top"

She kissed up his legs and passed his manhood that stood tall. Kayla made her way to his chest then his neck. As she kissed back and forth between his neck and lips, he could feel the warm of her wetness between her thighs. She slowly slid down onto his shaft and their connection was made. She rocked back and forth on him while laying chest to chest. His arms wrapped around her and his thrust went deeper. She could tell he was looking for the place of pleasure. The place that no other man could reach inside of her. They knew that once he was there her release would be intense but he loved finding that place over and over again. After twenty minutes of searching he was in familiar territory.

"Don't you hold back," he demanded.

She didn't. Her breathing changed and the moans increased. "Don't you hold back!" He held her closer and pushed her hips down further onto him. She couldn't hold back if she tried.

Between each breath she screamed, "Oh shit....yes....that's it......" That was one down for her and he was determine to make it a high five kind of night.

Now that the first one was out of the way Kayla could focus on him more.

She sat up on him and continued to rock back and forth. He looked up and could see her smile, his favorite curve. She looked at his face and knew she couldn't wait to have his son. She leaned forward and placed her hands on his chest. The grind of her hips massaged his dick. She started to talk to him. "You know I'm not ever going anywhere." He grabbed her hips as if to hold on for the ride, "Really, why not?"

"Cause I don't want to be anywhere else. No one else can do me like you do me. I love the way you love me." She slowly bounced on him while she leaned in and kissed his face. "Now enough of this mushy shit, fuck me however you want me."

"I want you just like this. On top and in control."

"Yes sir".

She continued to ride him and became more turned on at the idea of pleasing him. He felt her dripping down his legs and then it happened, pleasure turned into passion and they went to the next level. The rocking and gripping motions of her walls became more intense. Their breathing became harder. The sweat from her body made it easier to slide around on top of him.

Kayla loved on his dick and kissed his face. He held her waist and continued to push deep inside her. He had never been a lazy lover, just because she was on top didn't mean he wouldn't work. The combination of her motions and his thrust took her into number two but there were no whispers, only moans that grew louder, "Tyrone! .... Ooooh shit..... Don't stop...... Damn it"

He knew what that meant, he felt it. Slowly he sat up while her arms wrapped around his neck.

"Don't take him out" she said with panic in her voice.

"I'm not, what fun would that be." With one swift motion she was on her back and he was on top.

Her kitty was still purring as she felt him stroking, in and out of her. She didn't want to be a lazy lover but her legs were still shaking.

"Just wrap them around me and don't let go", he demanded

Her legs wrapped around him and his dick went deeper. Her back arched and curve her body towards his chest. He knew it was play time. He was a perfect fit inside of her and it was his playground. Knowing every dip and turn, Tyrone played hide and seek inside her. He was aware number three is hiding and it was his job to find it this time. She laid there calling his name while he played. Suddenly Tyrone pulled out. Kayla questioned, "Wait, what are you doing?"

Before an answer was provided, Tyrone's face disappeared and his tongue started to search for number three. Playing in front was no fun, he liked to slide around in the back. Tyrone held Kayla's legs over her head and he tasted the juices that had dripped from her valley. The stream flowed from her love fountain and he drank it all. The tip of his tongue tickled between her legs. Tyrone kissed and bit her inner thigh then demanded, "Lift that ass"

Kayla always did as she was told. She could feel soft kisses and nibbles on her cheeks. He was determined to find number three.

As Kayla's legs started to shake again he knew he was close. He continued to use one hand to hold it open while the other tapped lightly on her clit. Damn it, he found number three!

"Oh...my...gosh! What are you doing to me?" she screamed.

"What I am supposed to do." He was able to muffle out.

Vivid

Tyrone's tongue created a damn like effect that directed all of her into his mouth. He could taste her sweetness.

"Baby I need you to cum with me next time. I don't want to do this alone anymore" Kayla said as she tried to sit up.

"You have one more to get and then I promise to meet you there," he replied.

He got up from the bed watching her body in recovery. This was his time to show off his strength. Tyrone tossed her weak body around the bed.

He stood at the edge of the bed and pulled her to the edge. It was easy since she had no energy to resist it. "Flip over"

Again she did as she was told only this time not as quickly. Just as Kayla was able to place herself in the face down ass up position, Tyrone was back in his favorite place. He was licking her from behind and Kayla couldn't take it anymore. She tried to run across the bed but that was pointless.

"Now you know better than that." He said as he pulled her right back into his face and held her hips.

"Tyrone …..damn it…..you aren't playing fair."

"Whose is it?"

"Yours." Kayla seductively said.

"I do what I want with my stuff….whose is it?"

"It's yours baby."

"That's right. Give it to me."

She put a dip in her back and he couldn't resist. He stood up and slid right in. In and out while he changed his speed from slow and fast. She grabbed the sheets and tried to prop herself up on her elbows. He was not having that. "Face down…."

"Ass up," she replied.

He smiled, "That's my girl."

After she took it the way he liked to give it, Kayla started to feel her second wind come on. He knew it too. She started to throw it back just a little bit more with each stroke. "You feeling it now huh." Tyrone playfully asked.

"Dude you knew what you were doing?"

"Damn right it's mine and I know how it works."

She started to bounce on him while he stood behind her. "Oh really…" She bounced harder and faster, throwing it back with each stroke he sent. Then suddenly without warming she pulled away. He tried to grab her but it was too late she had turned her body around to put her face in front of his dick. Taking him into her mouth, she sucked her juices off of him and he was caught off guard. "Wait a damn minute," he stuttered as she licked all of herself off of him.

"Shut up and let me taste you now."

He stood for a minute then his knees were weak. He knew she was rested and isn't stopping until she got what she wanted. That had always been her way in everything. Sucking and slurping on him while he stood at the foot of the bed, she grabbed his sack and started to play. He braced himself by placing his hands on the bed. She knew he was almost there. He did too, he started to massage her lower back and her throat relaxed even more. He went deeper. She grabbed his waist and started to control the rhythm of his motion. She sucked faster and faster. He stopped massaging and held on. There was no holding back now. She softly mumbles, "Give it to me" as she started to drip from both sets of lips.

He couldn't stop it and her thirst was satisfied. His healthy diet of fruit for breakfast and snacks made it so much more enjoyable for her to drink him. He stood still while she finished drinking. He asked "you good."

"Are you, is the question," she asked as she swallowed all of his flavor. He smacked her ass and flipped her on her back. He started with her lips and licked down her body. Not in any rush nor in any one direction, he kissed and licks all over her mid-section. From one nipple to her belly button then back to her other nipple. He kissed around her neck and just loved on her body. She moved and moaned in ways to let him know that the forth was near.

"Tell me something good," he spoke between kisses.

"Cozy nights in."

"Yes, dinner was nice."

"I want dessert."

"Oh really?"

"Yes please" she said with a slight demand.

Kayla had hardly finished the words before her vagina was full of penis. The surprise and sudden thrust pushed out a moan that gripped the sheets. Slowly moving in and out of her, Tyrone looked deep into her eyes. In that moment keeping count no longer mattered and her satisfaction was the goal. She felt a change in his stroke and her body responded.

Chest to chest, she wrapped her arms around him. His arms were under her to pull her closer on to him. He dug deeper into her, it was time to plant his seed. She was watered and ready.

The room was filled with the scent of passion and the sounds of pleasure. She flexed her muscles and the grip of her walls drew him in deeper. With her legs wrapped around him, Tyrone started to whisper into her ear.

"I love you more than there are words."

"I love you too."

"Making you happy is my pleasure."

"And pleasing you makes me happy," she replied.

"I'm serious."

He started to kiss her again and tears fell from her eyes. There is no more to say. The moans and motions said it all. He rolled her over to be on top of him. She grinded her hips and sat up on him. He pulled her back down into his chest, kissed her ear and said "Stay close to me. Don't ever leave me."

"I won't," was her promise as she laid heart to heart.

He held her tight and she kissed his neck. Her smooth and steady rocking motion was bringing them closer to the final destination. The rocking slowly became a steady bounce and the pace increased. He could feel her and she could feel him. At that moment they moved together stroke by stroke. Grinding and bouncing to their own rhythm, they spoke in a true form of body language. Then it happened, the enjoyment of him being inside of her couldn't be over looked anymore and the pleasurable pressure was ready to erupt. He knew it and like a real man wanted to talk her through it.

"Are you going to give it to me?"

"Yes sir."

"Don't hold back on me. Cum on this dick."

She didn't have to be told twice. Tyrone could feel her contractions and the increase of her warmth. Kayla could feel his girth and the waterfall started to flow. Tyrone kept his promise and didn't leave her alone in this moment….. "That's it, that's my girl."

Vivid

Day and Night.....the next day

Being a boss is my destiny.
Organizing is a part of my passion.
Leader and director are included in my title.
But sitting at this conference table listening to reports and proposals aren't catching my attention as my mind continues to replay snap shots from last night.
When I answered your call yesterday, I could hear it in your hello.
To know your needs without an exchange of words is my specialty.
When we speak on the phone, you appreciate that I know all the right things to say and mean every word spoken.
I decided to close the door to my office and speak words that I knew would build you up for the night that was ahead.
Truth be told my soft moans not only enhanced my words but aroused my senses. The heat between my thighs was cooled off by my moisture.
Leaving all my titles in the office couldn't happen soon enough for me.
At home, you are the boss and I will never make you feel like less than that. Once I got home, the only thing that mattered was making the boss happy. I knew you had been in three different time zones in the pass 72 hours and couldn't wait to welcome you home.
Sharing laughs and talking about all that you had been involved with concerning you brand and business throughout the night was all the four play I needed.
Playing my role for you is never a problem for me.
Making you happy always makes me happy and I know my happiness is all that ever matters to you.
Sharing happiness all over the house last night was nice.
On the kitchen counter.
In the den on the sofa.
Sitting at the kitchen table.
Under the overhead shower in the master bathroom.
Starting in the bed of the master bedroom and ending on the floor of the hallway.
You make me oh so happy.
Today lunch time was planned as my refocus time.
I had planned on being ready for my two o'clock meeting and finishing the day off strong with no distraction.
I had done my daily walk through and was reviewing the proposal for the meeting.
Then I walked into this office with my head down in papers and took my seat behind this desk completely focused until that scent hit me......you must be my two o'clock.....

"Close and lock the door sir......"

Put In Work...

Kayla walked into Tyrone's house from the gym ready to shower and read herself to sleep. It had been a long day of venue walkthroughs and budget drafts. As she walked up the stairs she could hear Tyrone on the phone in his office. She decided not to bother him and went straight to the bedroom. She tried to respect his work time considering the many projects he had a hand in. She walked into the bedroom and prepared for a hot relaxing shower.

Kayla walked into her closet, grabbed her robe and then into the bathroom. She started the shower and walked over to the mirror to pull her hair up. As the water was running, she scrolled through her playlist for something to listen. The house was wired with speakers in every room and Tyrone had just taught her how to wirelessly stream her phone to his media system.

She stepped into the shower and started singing along with K. Michelle,

"Judge me, judge me all you want, I'm only human and I'm perfectly flawed..."

Two minutes later, Tyrone walked into the bathroom unnoticed and stood there for a moment looking through the foggy glass at his woman as she sang out loud. He opened the door and startled her by saying,

"I won't judge you I promise."

Kayla jumped, "You get on my nerves!" She screamed while slinging water in his direction.

He laughed then leaned in for a kiss and asked, "How was your day?"

"No complaints, I think they have decided on a location and now I need to call in some favors because the groom wants to surprise her with a celebrity solo during the reception."

"Who do they want?"

"Her favorite artist is Monica, I haven't seen or talked to her since that charity event in Atlanta a few months ago, but I'll see what I can do. I heard you on the phone when I came in. Didn't want to disturb you."

"It's cool, I thought I heard you come in. I was on the phone with Chrystal talking about the final color swatches for the new ties. I was about to call Ellis about these contracts for the property deal out south but this music started playing in the office."

"Aww baby I'm sorry I forgot about the exclusion button."

"You good, I hadn't moved from behind that desk in the last four hours. My eyes needed this break."

"Like what you see?", she asked as she slow danced in the shower.

"Hell yeah, I wish I could step in there with you."

Kayla smiled and seductively stood under the overhead shower. As the water slid down her breast and ass, Tyrone stepped back to take it all in.

"Get back to work sir. I'm going to finish in here and get in bed with a book."

"Swag on. I'll join you when I'm finished. I could use a good bedtime story."

She laughed as he slapped her ass then closed the shower door. The subtle tingle he left behind triggered on a new thought for Kayla.

She finished her shower and went into her nightly routine of lotion and pampering products. Once she was done, Kayla walked into Tyrone's closet then into her own. She had something else in mind instead of a bedtime story. She tipped toed quietly down the hallway, hoping not to disturb Tyrone in his office. He was so deep into paper work that he didn't hear her walk in.

Vivid

As she stood unnoticed in front of his desk, she cleared her throat and with a sultry voice whispered

"Mr. Johnson your appointment canceled. Can you squeeze me in?" Tyrone looked up to see her standing in front of his desk, wearing nothing but one of his neck ties and black pumps. She walked around his desk and stood directly in front of him.

Without saying a word he pulled her by the tie closer to him and started kissing her breast. His hands caressed her thighs as she massaged his shoulders. She stepped back from him and he leaned back in his chair. There had always been something about his bosshood that turned her on. She walked across the room slowly to the control panel for the media system. She turned her playlist back on. Tyrone grinned and said,

"I know that one, the sexy one right?"

"You know it."

"I like the sexy list," he said as he lowered his glasses from his face. He watched as she walked back towards him. The light in the room was dim and glowed off of her brown paper bag skin. As she walked, her hands traveled across her body. Her fingertips slipped into her mouth.

Kayla stood in front of him as he said "that's not what goes there". Slowly she fell to her knees and crawled closer to him. She gently undid his pants and started to suck his dick. Up and down her head moved and he felt her throat relax. He glided deeper into her mouth. Her moans grew more muffled and her mouth more full. She licked his sack while her hands played under his shirt on his chest. He could only take so much. It was then that he realized just how hungry he was.

"I haven't eaten all day," he suggestively commented.

"Well I am thirsty. I had a serious workout tonight," she managed to mumble out while sucking his shaft. He became more comfortable in his chair, who was he to deny her his juices. Her head moved in ways to increase her suction. He gripped the arms of his chair tighter and she knew her thirst would soon be quenched.

The moment that she could taste him, she drank all that he had to give. Before the last drop was swallowed, there was a change in her position. She went from being on her knees to laying on her back. His custom plush rug comforted her bare skin as he started to kiss down her body. Soon her legs were wrapped around his neck and there was an arch in her back that only he knew how to put there.

He was very hungry and she fed him all he could eat. She gazed through the floor to ceiling windows at the stars. His fingers teased her nipples and her eyes closed to capture that moment for a memory. As her sweetness coated his tongue then his lips and chin, she could feel his kisses coming back up her body.

Before her trembles could stop his dick was inside of her and her arms around his neck. Tyrone's strong thrust inside of her pushed out the orgasm that was still in progress. Intensely she came and he wrapped his arms around her. He licked her face as he rolled her over to be on top. The passion in the room increased as silence decreased.

Kayla started to ride out her pleasure and Tyrone thrusted slowly beneath her. Their eyes connected in a way that magnetically drew their lips together. The taste of her juices stained his beard.

"Damn I taste good," she announced.

"That's my girl."

Tyrone loved the fact that he had found a walking example of lady in the streets and freak in the sheets, so to speak. He could have her whenever and wherever.

Vivid

Kayla wanted to show her gratitude to Tyrone for always being the leader and supporter she needed. Grinding and sweating on top of him made Kayla's curvy frame slide with ease and his manly hands handled her motions. He controlled the pace and the next release. Their bodies were chest to chest and it was time to talk business.

"Tell me something good," he demanded softly.
"You inside of me is great."
"Really, tell me what's great about it."
"I love when you play inside me," she replied quietly with a steady bounce of her ass on his dick.
"What else?"
"I love it when your hands grip my....." before she could finish his hands where grabbing her hips and bringing her further down on his base.
"Yes....that right there......I love that," she said with a smile.
"Oh shit.....keep talking to me baby."
Kayla started kissing his neck, "your bosshood makes me wet."
"I love how you made up that word."
"Just for you. Your manhood feels good inside me, but your bosshood is what gets you inside of me."
"Is that it?" Tyrone asked.
"Of course not love, the way you hold me. Your continuous support and encouragement. How you deal with my moods."
"I'm your number one fan, always have been and always will be."
She loved it when he spoke to her like that.
He could feel her dripping down her thigh. "Thank you."
"For what love," Kayla asked as she kissed across his chest.
"For being what I need when I need it."
"No thanks needed."
Her hips started to move in a circular motion, "Your pleasure is mine."
Kayla sat up on him and allowed her walls to contract around the girth of his dick. She knew this would lead to an awesomely loud climax for them both. What she didn't know was he wasn't ready to get there yet. Tyrone sat up and her legs instinctively wrapped around him.
"Hold on", he instructed.
She did as told and he laid her back down on her back. He stayed inside of her, moving his pelvis in ways to hit spots that only he could. Her do as I'm told attitude went out the window as she screamed, "deeper daddy".
One quick push and then he pulled out.
"What in the hell are you doing now?"
"Being the boss."
He grabbed her by the hands and pulled her back up on her feet.
"Let me show you something," he said as he led her to the desk.
"Uh ok…" she agreed slightly confused.
Kayla walked over to his desk wondering what was so important that he had to stop what was going on in that moment.
"What am I looking for sir?"
Tyrone could hear she was now annoyed and was excited to change that with one quick motion.

Before Kayla could turn around she was bent over his desk and he was back inside her from behind.

"Say something else smart."

"That's it…..right there……damn it!"

"Who do you like I do?"

"Nobody" was the confession that escaped out of Kayla's mouth as her breathing became heavier.

She loved when he was back there. There was something about him holding her waist, controlling the depth and pace of their session that sent her body into overdrive. He would massage her lower back and caress her shoulders pulling her back onto him. He loved to watch her bounce on him from behind. Her softness was sexy. The paperwork that was laid across his desk reminded her that he was the boss and she took the opportunity to play on that.

She contracted her walls and started to grind on his dick while he stroked in and out from behind.

"Close the deal like only you can Mr. Johnson"

"We have to sign off on this together Ms. Jones"

"You have the pen……use it."

Kayla could feel his penis sliding in and out of her. He was preparing to leave his signature on what was his and only his. Tyrone could feel her grip tighten and he knew there was no other woman that could make him feel more like a man than her.

As the passion intensified and sensation brought them closer to eruption Tyrone decided he wanted to see her face. He pulled out.

"Wha…wait….what's wrong?" Kayla questioned with concern.

"I want to see your eyes," he answered with a kiss to her forehead.

He laid her down slowly on his desk and pulled her to the edge. He slid in at an angle that put her right back into the moment of cumming.. Tyrone took that opportunity to place her in his arms causing a deeper penetration. Kayla wrapped her legs around him and they started to move in-sync with one another.

"You know all I do is for us and our future," he whispered in her ear.

"And you know I appreciate it all." She kissed his face, "you are my king," then kissed his forehead, "and I am honored to be your queen." She took his face in her hands and kissed his lips, "let's build this kingdom…….together."

Reflection.....

I'm almost sleep but your scent lays across my pillow.
It causes a drift in my emotions.
I miss you.
I adjust my head and rearrange my pillow
but now that scent is dancing across my face.
It tickles my nose and whispers in my ears to my thoughts.
They replay a memory of time spent.
Like old black and white movies in color
I now see us in the past.
In the moment of closeness.
Surrounded by peace from my perspective.
I stay still to pause the moment there
afraid of losing it with the scent.
The scent remains but image has changed.
It's the future looking back at me.
I glaze at it and see....

Vivid

Long Distance.....

"I'll be home Friday night"

"How late Friday night?" was Kayla's question to Tyrone as they prepared to end their late night phone conversation.

"It's going to be more like early Saturday morning. I have a late meeting and the plane leaves at 9pm."

"So you will be home around two in the morning?"

"Yeah, that's about right."

It was Wednesday night and Kayla was more than ready to see Tyrone. He had been on the road for three months and they had never gone that long without seeing each other. It was never their intention to go that long without seeing each other but their work schedule never allowed a free weekend for alone time. There were a few weeks Tyrone found himself out of the country while Kayla was doing destination weddings on islands or beaches. Late night phone calls and quick online chats had become the normal. She had seen him from the neck up every other day for the last few months. She sent her share of pictures and 30 second videos to help keep him happy while he was gone but it was time for them to finally be side by side.

"Well go to bed love, don't you have that conference call in a few hours?" Tyrone lovingly asked.

Kayla turned to the clock on her nightstand and it read 1:17am.

"Yep, and they are Eastern Standard Time. I love you pooh"

"I love you too."

The call ended and her restless night began. Sleeping alone in a king size bed was nice the first few days but quickly became an old experience that she was ready to end.

As Kayla sat in her office located on the first floor of her townhouse, she read over emails that had come in overnight from potential clients and checked all the task for the day. Her conference call was scheduled for 6am central standard time and she had about ten minutes before it started. She read the online inquiries from her website and started checking her calendar to schedule new client consultations.

Thursday mornings were check in days for all of her event managers. She had one big event happening over the weekend in Miami and this conference call would be the final check in for all the on-site coordinators. Kayla dialed in and entered the code for the call. Once the line was connected she wasted no time starting the call.

"Good morning good people, how are you all doing?"

There was a pause, then a moment of silence and then she heard the first response. "Good morning Ms. Jones."

It was Kelly, one of Kayla's event assistance. "It's just me this morning."

"Where is Diana?" Kayla asked with concern in her voice.

"She is still sick, but I have everything under control."

That didn't sit well with Kayla. This event was a reoccurring event and the company name was on the line if there were any mishaps.

"I will be there tonight." Kayla quickly responded.

Kelly insisted that everything would be ok but Kayla's mind was made up.

As she headed to her bedroom, her cell phone rang. She answered.

"Yes sir?" It was Tyrone.

"What are you doing?"
"Packing."
"For what?" he asked.
"I have to fly out tonight to Miami for this event. Diana is still sick and while Kelly is good I just don't want to leave all this up to her so soon. I will be back Sunday morning."
"And I will be leaving out Sunday morning."
"I thought you were home for a week."
"That's what I was calling about. I am coming in tonight because there has been a change with a few deadlines and I want to close a deal or two early. Ellis is already in Los Angeles and I need to meet with him on Monday morning. So I'll be back in the city tonight around 10."
"My flight leaves at six."
There was a slight pause then Tyrone said, "Well when you are done just fly out to Los Angeles Sunday morning instead of going home."
"I will have to see if Nicole is open Monday, I have three consultations that day. And I honestly don't want to fly in and out of Los Angeles within a 24 hour time frame."
Another moment of silence.
"I'll see what I can do Ty," she promised.
"We will work it out," he replied with confidence.
They continued to have small talk while Kayla packed and then it ended like most of their day time conversations do.
"Well I'm walking into this meeting love I'll call you tonight."
"Alright, love you Ty."
"Love you too."
Kayla spent the next three hours around the house packing and working. Her car arrived and as she got in, there on the back seat sat a dozen roses with a card attached. It read "We do this now so we can do whatever later. I love you T" It brought a smile to her face but being in his arms would have placed a smile in her heart. She missed him a lot.
Once she landed and turned her phone back on, she was greeted by multiple alerts but she only looked for one. As she scrolled through her text messages she found what she was looking for.
"I know you are on the plane. I just came out the meeting and am headed to the airport myself. I have a 30 minute layover in Atlanta around eight. Call me when you land."
Kayla looked at the time on the top of her phone and realized that she had about seven minutes before it was 8:30. She called his phone and instantly got his voicemail. Sad that she had missed him, she left a simple message, "I made it safe love. Call me when you make it in. Love you"
Kayla arrived to the hotel and before she was able to check in completely she was met by one of the on-site assistants. "Call everyone down to the conference room and meet me there in 20 minutes."
The following day was full of follow ups and final counts. Meetings with clients and vendors back to back left very little time to talk on the phone with Tyrone. When she was able to get a minute to herself, he would be unavailable. Kayla was thankful that they had mastered the art of text communication very early in their relationship. It wasn't until 2:15 am that she was able to hear his voice.
"How is everything going down there?"

Vivid

Kayla laid still on her side of the bed with her phone on the pillow next to her. He was on speaker and the room was silent.
"I have to be up at 5:45am"
"What time will things get started?"
"The show starts at 6pm and then the after party starts around 11. There is a cocktail reception between the two."
"Very busy day huh?"
"Not really." Kayla nonchalantly replied.
"Did you talk to Nicole?"
"She has to show four venues on Monday. I didn't even bother calling her. Once I pulled up the calendar I saw it and realized everyone is busy that's why I ended up with the consultations in the first place."
"Well I will figure it out, get some rest and call me when you get done tomorrow night."
"I will."
They ended their call and before she could plug her phone in, Kayla was sleep.
The sun wasn't up yet and her phone started ringing, "Hello."
"Good morning my dear."
"Good morning sir."
Kayla smiled at his voice and was thankful that Tyrone had taken time out to call her before the day got too busy.
"Let me pray for you before you walk out the door."
Kayla stood in front of the door with her bags in hand and bowed her head. He prayed for her covering and strength and she walked out the door with peace that only comes from within.
Seventeen hours later, the event had finally ended for her at 12:30 am and she was in her car on the way to the hotel when she was able to call him back.
He answered, "Hello."
"Hey there."
"What's up, how did everything go?"
"It went well. I left Kelly in charge of clean up and am on the way back to the room."
"Cool, what time is your flight tomorrow?"
"I have a late check out and will be at the airport around two."
"I pushed my flight back so I will see you in the airport."
"Yay" Kayla faintly said with a touch of excitement in her voice and a small smile on her face.
They had small talk while she relaxed in the back of the car with her eyes closed.
"How far are you from the hotel?"
She opened one of her eyes and looked out the window, "maybe ten minutes"
"That's cool. Did I tell you how much I miss you?"
"No but I'm sure it's not as much as I miss you."
"I would beg to differ but I'll show you better than I can tell you."
"How would you show me?"
"Well I would start by taking your hand and leading you to a nice warm bath. After all you just told me about this event you deserve it. I would massage your shoulders and say sweet shit in your ear."
"Really.....sweet shit?"
"You know what I mean. "

Vivid

They laughed together and finally the car stopped in front of the hotel. She sat there waiting for the driver to open her door. While she waited Tyrone said, "your turn."

"For what?"

"To tell me about all the things you would do to show me how much you missed me."

Since she was caught off guard she simply said, "You aren't ready."

Tyrone opened her car door and said, "Try me."

Being totally paralyzed by shock and surprise Kayla sat in the back of the car and cried. Tyrone had planned to make this night even more romantic and got in the car with her. "Driver, would you please?"

The driver understood and without another word they were driving to nowhere, with the partition up. Kayla was hit with a new burst of energy. He was finally next to her. She could finally feel him and be in the space she called the nook. It was her space. When she was in that space nothing else mattered. When in the nook all troubles were nonexistent

"Tell me something good."

"This nook of mine," Kayla answered as she melted into place.

Tyrone kissed her forehead and pulled her in close. As comfort covered her, Tyrone took full advantage of being next to her. His hands began to search her body for places he had missed for the last few months.

"What are you doing Tyrone?"

"Trying to warm up my hands, the air is on and they are cold."

She smiled at his subtle sexiness.

His fingertips were cool to the touch but glided across her thigh softly. The sensation sent a tingle up her spine. There was something in this touch that awakened her on the inside. She sat up and looked him in his eyes.

"I missed you," she said followed by a simple kiss to his cheek.

"Did you really?"

"More than words could ever express."

"Can I tell you something?'"

"Anything," Kayla reassured him.

"This is the first time in weeks that I feel at peace."

"Me too."

She leaned in to kiss him on the forehead and then on his cheek. Unable to control her desire for him she started kissing his neck. The space in the car made it easy for her to change her position. As she straddled on his lap, kissing his neck, Tyrone wrapped his arms around her waist so his hands could rest on her ass. Kayla had missed this feeling of passion and protection. She could feel the growth in his pants and a warmth between her legs. "Take me back to the room please."

"When it's time to return we will."

"I don't want to wait for this any longer."

He kissed her lips and said, "Patience my love."

"You know I have none," she said as she sat back down on the seat next to him with a noticeable attitude.

"Don't be like that. Don't change the mood of the moment," Tyrone requested as he kissed her hand.

With a deep sigh, Kayla laid back and looked out the window. They were approaching the beach.

Vivid

As the car pulled into a parking spot, Tyrone asked Kayla a question.
"Do you trust me completely?"
"Of course."
"Let's go walk on the beach."
"Really?"
"Yes....just us."
"It could be just us in the room."
"When we leave here I promise we are heading straight to the room."
"You have to carry me on your back on the way back to the car."
"I can do that."
Kayla grins and gestures for him to get out, "Let's go."
They exited the car and walked towards the shore.
"I don't think I have ever walked on the beach this late. And all the stars can be seen. It's so beautiful out here."
Tyrone looked up in the sky, "yeah there are a lot of stars up there."
"You ok?"
"Always, just thinking about the time."
"This was your idea dude."
"I know, that's not what I meant by time."
"Care to share?" Kayla asked while dragging her feet in the warm sand.
"When I say time I meant in our lives. Since I have known you we have always been short on time. Be it due to work or family or whatever."
"Well, this is the life that we talked about hun. You being the multiple business owner/ boss man, while I plan all the fabulous events in the country. Eventually a few around the world."
"I know," Tyrone said as he nudged Kayla in her side.
She laughed and punched him in the arm. As the humor died down, Kayla looked up and saw candle light close in the distance. "What did you do man?"
"Figured you would be tired. I thought it would be nice to rest for a minute, before I have to carry you back to the car."
Kayla giggles to herself and then slaps his arm, "You think you are so smooth. Whatever, I'm not impressed."
"I know better than that. I know I'm one smooth ass dude."
"I guess."
The two of them walked up to a candlelit cabana that had a full size hammock underneath it. Next to the hammock was a small table with chocolate covered strawberries and her favorite drink. Tyrone laid down in the hammock and took Kayla by the hand. He looked up at her and could see the golden brown tones of her cheeks in the flicker of the flames that surrounded them. "Come here."
Kayla took her time and laid down slowly next to him in the hammock. They rocked back and forth while looking up through the sheer fabrics of the cabana top. The stars were bright and the breeze was pleasant. The ocean was the background soundtrack for their moment. Kayla laid next to him with one leg stretched across him. Tyrone's arm turned into her pillow and the heat between her legs kept him warm.
"Are we sleeping out here tonight?"
"I hadn't planned on it. Just wasn't ready to go in yet."
"How did you pull this off?" Kayla questioned.

Vivid

Tyrone explained that he had called Diana a few days before and explained what he wanted to make happen.

"So that heffa isn't sick?" Kayla sarcastically questioned.

"Nope. She was out here setting this up."

"How long have you been here?"

"My plane landed around seven."

Kayla just laid there.

"What's wrong," Tyrone asked.

"Nothing is wrong, just thinking about it all."

"All of what? Talk to me."

Kayla had realized what he meant about the time of their lives that they had dreamed about for the past six years.

"We are so close to the life that we dreamed about. There are still a few things we are working out but for the most part this is it."

"What would you say is missing?"

"You already know what I think it is, marriage."

"I just wanted to hear you say it."

They had been dating for six years and while there was no intention of leaving the relationship, Kayla knew marriage was something that she desired in her life. Being a wife and mother was definitely a part of her future. The two of them had their share of issues in the beginning and she was sure that they weren't meant to be. Then life happened and once the dust settled they were still standing.

As they swayed slowly, Tyrone started to whisper in her ear.

"I appreciate your patience with me."

"I thank you for loving me, even when I was unfair to you."

She kissed him and his fingers tipped down the front of her skirt. She was so into the taste of his lips that she was pleasantly surprised when he found the wet and warm spot between her legs. His thick fingers slid in and out with ease. He went deeper with each stroke. She started biting his lip and running her fingers up and down his manly arms, "I'm ready for you to carry me back."

"Not yet," he stated.

Soon the sounds of her moans grew louder than the crashing of the waves to the shore. As Tyrone felt her melt in his hands, he slowed his motions and said "let's go"

Careful not to flip the hammock, they got up and she climbed onto his back. With her arms around his neck and her legs weaved between his arms, Kayla laid her head on his shoulder and closed her eyes. She imagined herself being carried away by a giant and with every step she could feel the earth shake beneath them.

The ride back to the hotel ended quickly. As they exited the car, Tyrone took Kayla by the hand yet again and looked at her. He kissed her and asked, "Are you ready?"

"For bed."

"That will be a part of it."

She giggled to herself as they walked into the lobby.

The stillness of the lobby echoed their footsteps and a soft greeting from behind the front desk.

"Good evening Mr. Johnson and Mrs. Jones."

Vivid

They walked towards to the elevators and Tyrone pressed the up button. As they stepped onto the elevator, he pressed the button for the 18th floor.

"Baby I'm on the 15th floor," Kayla said as she went to press what she thought was the correct button.

"Not anymore."

"Man, what have you done?"

"They knew I was coming into town, I got my regular room."

"I guess."

She laid her head on his chest and rested for the moment. Then asked, "Did they move my stuff to your room?"

"Yep."

"Thank you"

"No problem."

As they exited the elevator, Tyrone could sense just how tired Kayla really was. He opened the door for her and allowed her to walk in first. The room was covered with white orchids and peonies, her favorite flowers. The aroma of her Bedroom Kandi candles filled the room.

"You are really showing out tonight love."

"I don't know what you are talking about," Tyrone said with a sense of confidence that Kayla loved.

She kissed his face and then walked further into the room.

"Give me a minute, you relax your pretty little self over there on the couch."

Tyrone walked away as Kayla laid down on the couch. One minute turned to five and five to ten. Fifteen minutes later, she was awaken from her sudden and deep sleep.

"Come with me."

Without question she took his hand and followed him. He led her into the bathroom and she stood in awe. He had filled the tub and all that could be seen where bubbles. She stood there for a second and then turned to face him. Before she could say thank you he turned her back around to face the tub. He took full control and begun to kiss her neck. Her eyes closed and her mind drifted. His hands caressed her body and slid up to her shoulders. Massages to the top of her back made her unprepared for his next move. He unbuttoned her shirt and let it drop to her feet. Followed by her skirt then bra. She stood in only her panties and Tyrone placed his fingers inside them and tickled her lips.

"Step in the tub", he said as he nibbled on her ear.

As she lifted her leg, he started to slide her panties off. She stepped into the tub and began to sit down.

"Wait a minute," he commanded.

She stood in the tub completely naked. Tyrone stepped back and looked at her body. "Ok, do it slowly."

With a smile on her face, Kayla turned to the side and slowly bent over. Resting her hands on the side of the tub, she seductively sat in the water and laid back. As her body started to disappear under the bubbles, Tyrone got on his knees and dipped a soft body sponge in the water. Starting with her shoulders he washed her from head to toe. She laid in the moment and let him have his way.

Being completely relaxed and in the moment of it all, she didn't realize that he had left the room. Kayla laid there for five more minutes and then proceeded to dry off. She wrapped herself

Vivid

in a black silk robe that was laying on the counter and walked back into the bedroom. Tyrone was laying in the bed asleep. There were pedals on the floor and the candles were still flickering in the background. She walked slowly towards the bed and whispered his name.

"Tyrone?.....Ty......," there was silence.

Kayla returned to the restroom and finished her nightly routine. She always applied her lotion from the top down and as she bent over to lotion her legs, she heard, "Don't move."

She peeked behind her while remaining in a bent over position and saw Tyrone standing in the doorway.

"Can I finish?" she asked.
"In a minute. I am enjoying this view."
"I would really like to join you in that bed."
"Oh you will, eventually."
Tyrone smacked her ass and walked away, "continue."

Kayla giggled and finished what she was doing. She walked back to the bed with her robe undone. Tyrone laid in the bed watching her hips sway side to side. The silkiness of the robe flowed behind her and reflected the glimmer of the candles.

She crawled into bed and laid next him.
"Thank you for a very relaxing evening."
Tyrone replied, "You deserved it," and kissed her forehead.
She was more than rested and was ready to show him just how thankful she was…..

A memory.....

She laid on her stomach in her bed wearing only a simple black tank and thin strapped thong. Thinking about the last few days of her life, she had been blessed in so many ways but couldn't fully enjoy her excitement because her other half was so far gone. She knew it would come but was never completely prepared for it. Laying in her thoughts, she started to drift between reality and fantasy not really knowing the difference between the two. She could suddenly feel him in the room. His cologne filled the air. Afraid to open her eyes for fear of the truth being a dream she laid in silence until his touch warmed her shoulder. The comfort of his hand said relax and that's what she did. Soon both of his hands were rubbing away the past 48 hours of their history and her focus was the present. With eyes closed and a smile on her face she laid in his protection.

There was never a word spoken but everything was understood. He kissed the back of her neck and felt her back arch in pleasure. It said I'm sorry and she forgave him. He kissed down her back to the curves of her hips. Watching her body's silhouette dance in the candle light he decided to tango with her. She flipped over to her back and he held himself above her while his middle met hers. She desired to dance on his pole and he allowed it. Slowly pushing inside her space, the silence was broken and they both moaned out of relief. The buildup of weeks was released. Her legs being wrapped around him added to her grip as he stroked his way through her waters. Her rivers flowed and he enjoyed the swim. She created the waves and he held on for the ride. Whispers of love escaped from her lips and he acknowledged he heard them with deeper strokes. Coming to the shore together made for a very wet arrival.

She laid for a minute while the wave subsided. Pulling herself together, she opened her eyes only to realize she was alone and her finger tips wet.

To Reconcile....

She laid on his side of the bed and thought about how long it had been since he laid there. Her actions of the past were influenced by his past actions which impacted their present. The future she had envisioned for them was slowly being erased but the picture was still clear to her. "This version of us needs to end and if it's supposed to be we'll start new" were words that played over in her head as she laid in his spot.

Kayla was missing how he would wake her with a morning message and converse with her all night. He was her sounding board and now all her thoughts remained trapped. As she laid on her stomach and the memories of them escaped through the tears she cried she felt something.

A familiar touch to the nape of her neck. "You miss me?" It was him. He had snuck in with silence. She looked up at him,
"You're here......for real?"
"Should I leave?" Tyrone asked.
"No...."
She sat up and looked at him.
"You miss me?"
"Yes....." she whispered with the increase of tears.
"I'm here don't cry"

He took her face and kissed her lips. The sound of sadness stopped but the tears still fell. He gently wiped a falling tear then kissed her face. "Please stop". He kissed her cheek. She closed her eyes. He kissed her forehead.

"Thank you for coming" she said to the large shadow that sat at the edge of the bed and was formed by the moonlight.

"I missed you" he said as he got more comfortable.

Before she could question why he changed his mind about them, she was in his arms. Oh how she had longed for this place. It was a place that no other man had ever provided. Her nook. Her space. It was her protection, her security, her comfort, and her warmth.. By his side and in his arms was a perfect fit for her.

As if the last month of no communication had never happened he
asked her "what's on your mind?"
She was scared to answer. What if honesty was too much right now? What if she ran with the inch and still came up short? Safe answer,
"Nothing new".
She was telling the truth and hoped it was enough for him to understand. When she realized he hadn't responded she asked the same. His deep breath shifted her position slightly closer to him.

"I'm wondering if you will ever truly forgive my mistake. Can you ever trust me in a way that will let us really move on from here? Why keep going through it all over and over again?"

She had always asked those question to herself but now he's asking them out loud. That had never happened.

"I don't know anymore." She replied with eyes fixed to the ceiling. They laid in the faint sounds of infomercials.

Vivid

"So what now" she asked.

"I honestly don't know anymore."

She turned her back to him but remained in his arms. He started to rub her back. Without a word he knew she was hurting. They had always had a connection that didn't always require words. He turned to face her back and she could feel the coolness of his breathe on her neck.

She needed his kiss but didn't dare ask. There was no need. His arms wrapped around her tightly and then he said, "I love you. Didn't plan on it but I do. I don't want to lose you. I want to make this work. I want to show you this time. You are all I want." He kissed her ear. "That seals my word"

She adjusted herself to be more comfortable in his arms. "Love you too."

The curves of her body were in alignment with his straight parts. They laid in the heat but he remained cool until she said "make love to me" He rolled her on top of him and smiled "no problem"

She laid on top of him chest to chest and he took full control. He held her face and pulled her in for the most passionate kiss that sent a pulse through her body. She was alive again. He could feel her coming to life. While she started to kiss his neck she used her hands to finish undressing him. He caressed her thighs as she slid slowly onto his lovestick....

Vivid

Personal message from the author:

First let me thank you for taking time out of your day or night to read this small expression of my thoughts. I have always enjoyed writing and never thought that one day someone would actually want to read it. I also enjoy most things erotic and exotic. I have been blessed to combine my passions
I would love to get your feedback about this. Bad or good, every review is greatly appreciated.
You can do so by visiting my Facebook page. Southern Lady Books.
Again I thank you for your time and attention and I love you all. I promise I do.
Sincerely,
Jenae'

www.ingramcontent.com/pod-product-compliance
Ingram Content Group UK Ltd.
Pitfield, Milton Keynes, MK11 3LW, UK
UKHW022213230426
12048UKWH00016BA/825